The Magic School
Bus Takes A
Dive

Joanna Cole

Scholastic's
The Magic School Bus®

TAKES A DIVE
A Book About Coral Reefs

SCHOLASTIC INC.
New York   Toronto   London   Auckland   Sydney

From an episode of the animated TV series
produced by Scholastic Productions, Inc.
Based on *The Magic School Bus* books
written by Joanna Cole and illustrated by Bruce Degen.

TV tie-in adaptation by Nancy White and illustrated by Ted Enik.
TV script written by Jocelyn Stevenson.

ISBN 0-590-18723-6

12 11 10 9 8 7 6 5 4 3 2 1   8 9/9 0 1 2/0

Printed in the U.S.A.   23
First Scholastic printing, November 1998

2/99
ENF 536 COL
$6.99

I'll never forget the time our class project was to build a model of a coral reef in a fish tank.

I thought it would be just an ordinary project. With Ms. Frizzle as our teacher, I should have known better.

According to my research, a coral reef is found in a shallow part of the ocean. It's made by tiny animals, and it's really alive!

Ms. Frizzle said everything we put into the coral reef had to be done by partners. We were admiring our work, when Wanda came in with a treasure chest she had made for the reef. Dorothy Ann looked really upset. She and Wanda were supposed to make something together.

Just then a surprising thing happened. Well, nothing
is really surprising in Ms. Frizzle's class.

Good morning, class!

s soon as Ms. Frizzle saw Wanda's
asure chest in the fish tank, she
d, "Hmm, that reminds me
omething." Then she started
nmaging through her closet.

Ah! Here it is!

Finally, out came the Friz waving an old, crumpled-up piece of paper. "My great-great-great-great-great-great-great-great-great-great-grandfather Red Beard's treasure map!" she announced. "Red Beard was the pirate in the family."

"Wow! A real pirate!" said Wanda. "And a map of a real place — with a real coral reef! Is the treasure real, too, Ms. Frizzle?"
"Well, Wanda," said the Friz, "there's only one way to find out."

TO THE BUS!

Did I forget to mention that our class takes a lot of field trips?
And one other thing — it's about our school bus. Let's put it this way — the oil isn't the only thing that gets changed now and then.

Pretty soon, we could see an island in the distance.
"Coral reef, ho!" Ms. Frizzle announced. "We're here! Drop anchor!"

We didn't see any coral reef, of course, because a coral reef is underwater. And that was exactly where we were going! "Partners, everyone! Two by two, please," ordered Ms. Frizzle.

Wanda wanted to find the coral reef — and the treasure — by herself, but Ms. Frizzle said Wanda had to be D.A.'s partner.

What good is a partner, anyway?

Without a partner, you could get into deep trouble!

Being underwater didn't stop D.A. from giving one of her lectures. "According to my research," she said, "there's not much food and no shelter for fish in deep ocean water. That's why we're not seeing any fish around here."

"But there are lots of different kinds of fish living in a coral reef," added Ralphie.

So, where's the reef?

All I see is a lot of deep water.

Then Wanda made an exciting discovery. An old chain on the ocean floor matched up exactly with a dotted line on the map — and the line led straight to the treasure. Now Wanda really wanted to go solo!

Ms. Frizzle gave Liz a signal, and before we knew it, some of us were hermit crabs! Others were sea anemones — weird animals that look like plants. Ms. Frizzle was an anemone, too.

We all had our problems. Anemones — like plants — can't move. And hermit crabs don't have it so great, either. Big animals — say, a big fish or an octopus — want to eat them! But the hermit-crab kids found they were safe as long as they stuck close to the sea-anemone kids.

We even found out that a hermit crab can carry a sea anemone on its back. The crab gets protection, and the sea anemone gets transportation!

Wanda and D.A. followed the chain almost to the treasure. But suddenly, the chain went into a tiny hole in a rock.
"How are we going to get through that teeny-tiny space?" Wanda asked.

Now there's a question worth diving into, Wanda!

Then the Friz gave Liz that same signal again. What made me think another surprise was coming?

"At least I can move," said Wanda. "But what are we now, Ms. Frizzle?"
"We're pistol shrimp, Wanda!" said Ms. Frizzle.
"What about us, Ms. Frizzle?" asked Tim. "I think we're some kind of fish."
"You're right, Tim," said Ms. Frizzle. "You're goby fish."

Ms. Frizzle told us that pistol shrimp use their claws to dig holes. What's the point of digging holes? We were about to find out.

Wanda started using her claws to dig a tunnel to the treasure. She was doing great, when she found she had one problem. Pistol shrimp don't see too well.

I can't see anything!

The goby-fish kids found that they had a problem, too. A big shark was headed straight for them!

The goby-fish kids headed straight for the holes the pistol-shrimp kids had been digging. Those holes made perfect hiding places. And it was a good thing for the pistol shrimp, too. If it hadn't have been for the goby fish, they never would have seen the shark!

Now we were getting the idea that this whole field trip was about partners working together. Thanks to the pistol shrimp, we could follow the chain through the tunnel. And thanks to the goby fish, we could see where we were going.

When we were through the tunnel, Ms. Frizzle turned some of us into sharks. She turned the rest of us into remoras. Remoras are fish that eat little animals called copepods. The copepods live on the skin of sharks. So the remoras get a tasty snack, and the sharks get a good cleaning!

A remora has little suction cups on its body that let it attach itself to the skin of a shark. So off raced the shark-and-remora partners to see who would reach the treasure first.

Suddenly, the reef started to look different.

"Hey, what's wrong with the reef?" said D.A. "Look over there. It looks almost . . . dead!"

Wanda said, "Never mind that, the treasure's in there! Let's get it!" Wanda has a one-track mind when it comes to treasure.

Get treasure . . . get treasure . . . get treasure . . .

Wanda and D.A. pushed and pulled, twisted and tugged, but the treasure chest was too heavy to move.

Then something awful happened. A big piece of the reef broke off! The whole dead-looking part started to crumble right on top of Wanda and D.A. — and the treasure!

Luckily for Wanda and D.A., they were okay. I guess the Friz figured enough was enough, because she signaled Liz again and we turned back into human kids.

The bus was with us again, looking just a little different from before. It brought us these great mega-magnifiers — special magnifying glasses that would make everything look much MUCH bigger.

What do you know — we're humans again!

In my old school, we were *always* humans.

We all started inspecting different parts of the reef with our mega-magnifiers.

ow I know why they ay the reef is alive.

This is a BIG surprise!

"Hey, look at this," said Tim. The reef is made of tiny little nimals!"

"Bingo, Tim," said the Friz. A coral reef is really a mestone skeleton built by ttle animals called polyps. nd they're building new coral ll the time."

"Hold on," said Tim. "I think these polyps over here have something the ones in the sick part don't have."

"Right again, Tim," said Ms. Frizzle. "Tiny plants called algae live inside the polyps. Algae make up that scummy green stuff you see on top of a pond."

"So are polyps and algae partners, too?" asked Wanda.

"Righteously reasoned, Wanda!" said the Friz. "Algae give off wastes that help the polyps make the reef. And the algae get a nice safe place to live — away from all those hungry fish."

Polyps have no color. It's the algae that give color to the reef.

"But, Ms. Frizzle," said Ralphie, "how come the polyps on the sick part of the reef don't have algae partners?"

"According to my research," said D.A., "if the water around a coral reef becomes polluted, the polyps get rid of their algae partners."

We dug up the treasure chest. It was made of some kind of metal. Ms. Frizzle told us it was copper, and copper pollutes water! "Hit it, Liz!" she shouted, and the bus lifted the chest up to the surface.

Next, our bus WHOOSHED up all the polluted water from around the sick coral. Clean water flowed into that part of the reef.

We could see that the polyps were taking in algae again.

The coral polyps have algae again.

The partnership is working!

ormally, it would take hundreds
ears for those tiny polyps to
ld up the reef again. But since
en was anything normal with
Frizzle around?

Let's speed things up a little.
Take it away, Liz!

efore we knew it, the reef was completely built up.

The polyps and the
algae did it!

They rebuilt
the reef!

Safely back in the classroom, we opened the chest.
Inside was a portrait of Ms. Frizzle's relative, Red Beard,
and a model of his ship.

"Ah yes, Red Beard,"
said the Friz as she
hung the pirate's pictur
on the wall.

"He had no idea that his treasure chest
would someday pollute the reef. He would
thank you for pulling it out, if he only knew!"

Ask the Producer

Kid Caller: Is it true that most animals have partners?

Producer: No. Partnerships usually happen only when each animal does better as a result. Sometimes, only one animal benefits, like the coral-reef crab. It lives under the spines of the black sea urchin. The crab gets some useful protection. But the urchin doesn't get anything out of it.

Kid Caller: Is a coral reef really alive?

Producer: You bet! Millions of polyps live together, building the reef, year after year.

Kid Caller: Do reefs really get sick like you showed?

Producer: Yes, they do, for lots of different reasons, including pollution.

Kid Caller: I think that coral reefs are some of the world's great treasures. We have to do what we can to protect them.

Producer: You got that right, partner!

Magic School Bus, producer speaking.

An Outdoor Adventure for Parents and Kids

A fancy word for partnerships in nature is *symbiosis*, which really means "living together." If you take a walk outside, you're bound to find at least one or two more examples of plants or animals that live together. Here's what you might find:

- **Lichens** Examine some rocks. Do any of them have a dry, moldy-looking growth on them? If so, you're probably looking at *lichens* (LIE kenz). A lichen is a combination of two plants. The outer green, brown, yellow, or gray layer is a *fungus* (like a mushroom), and the greenish layer underneath is *algae*. Algae make their own food but need a lot of water to live. A fungus can't make food but can hold lots of water. So the fungus gets food, the algae get water, and the two live together happily as a lichen.

- **Livestock** Do you live in an area where people keep *livestock*, such as chickens, cows, horses, or sheep? Livestock and humans are partners! The animals get food and shelter, and the humans get wool, milk, eggs, and other useful products.

- **Pets** Humans and their pets are partners. We give our pets food, shelter, and love. In return, we get a friend, playmate, or just an interesting or beautiful animal to look at. Some pets do useful jobs for people. Dogs act as watchdogs and guide dogs for people who are blind. Cats keep mice away from people's houses and barns.

Good luck in your symbiosis search!

Ms. Frizzle